The Transfigured Hart

The
Transfigured Hart

———❧❧———

BY JANE YOLEN

Illustrated by Donna Diamond

Thomas Y. Crowell Company • New York

Library of Congress Cataloging in Publication Data
Yolen, Jane H.   The transfigured hart.
SUMMARY: A boy and a girl become convinced that the
white deer they discover in the woods is a unicorn.
[1. Unicorns—Fiction.   2. Magic—Fiction]
I. Diamond, Donna, ill.   II. Title.
PZ7.Y78Tr   [Fic]   75-2377
ISBN 0-690-00736-1

1   2   3   4   5   6   7   8   9   10

for
DAVID,
who has always indulged my passion
for unicorns

Other books by Jane Yolen

THE BIRD OF TIME
THE GIRL WHO LOVED THE WIND
THE WIZARD ISLANDS
THE BOY WHO HAD WINGS
THE GIRL WHO CRIED FLOWERS AND OTHER TALES
RAINBOW RIDER
THE MAGIC THREE OF SOLATIA
THE SEEING STICK

The Sages say truly that two animals are in this forest: one glorious, beautiful and swift, a great and strong deer; the other an unicorn. . . . If we apply the parable of our art, we shall call the forest the body: . . . The Unicorn will be the spirit at all times. The deer desires no other name but that of the soul. . . . He that knows how to tame and master them by art, to couple them together, and to lead them in and out of the forest, may justly be called a Master.

—from Abraham Lambsprink's
On the Philosophers' Stone,
a rare Hermetic tract

• one •

The hart lived in a thicket close by a shimmering pool. He had been born in that thicket on a spring morning before the sun had quite gained the sky.

As soon as he was born, his mother had sensed something wrong. She licked off his birth wrapping. The sheaths fell off his hooves. But the doe nuzzled her fawn with a hesitant motion, puzzling out his peculiarity.

He was an albino, born weak and white on that clear spring day. His eyes were pink and his nose a mottled pink, too.

After a few minutes, the doe was satisfied. The fawn would live. He was different, but he would live.

So the white hart was born, and so he grew.

By the time he had reached his fifth year, and had dodged the pack of dogs that ran in the woods and, in season, the hunters as well, he was a wise and wily beast. He knew the best runs to the water. He could paw down the snow to the shoots that winter had left and find the sweet early spring grass.

No hunters in the area had actually identified the albino. Or if they had noticed a flash of white, they had not known him for what he was. For the white hart was a loner. He chose a solitary existence, never joining—even in the rutting season—the small herds that lived in Five Mile Wood.

He spent much of his time in the thicket of twenty-two trees close by the shimmering pool. And he lay, mute and gleaming, under a wild apple tree a good part of each day.

· *two* ·

Richard Plante was a loner, too. He had read a lot for a twelve-year-old. At first he read because he was so sick and there was nothing else to do in the great house where he lived, the only child among adults.

Richard read about giants and kings, about buried treasure and ghosts, about gods and heroes far away in place and time and some near enough for memory. His wall was papered with the lists of his reading, neatly arranged by subject and author in a secret code that only he understood.

Richard had read in his bed, mostly, since that was where he had seemed condemned to spend much of his early childhood. But even after he got better and was allowed to run about several hours a day and urged to play with children his own age, the reading habit stayed with him. He read in his bed, still, though his room was outfitted with two generous reading chairs with a table and lamp between them. And when he was pronounced entirely well from the rheumatic fever that had kept him in bed, the loner habit stayed with him, too.

Rather than being with other children when the adults urged him out of doors, Richard preferred to take a book and make his way deep into Five Mile Wood. When he could find a comfortable spot lined with soft leaves, a mossy place by a stream, an outdoor bed, Richard would lie down and read. He read in great gulps, devouring his books with an appetite his aunt would have preferred he show at the table. And he retained almost all that he read, his mind a ragbag of facts that he forced into mental lists.

After several hours had passed, Richard would tuck his book into his shirt and head for home. He would run the last hundred yards or so. That way he would be just enough out of breath to allow his aunt to assume he had been following doctor's orders and playing outdoors with neighborhood friends.

It was after dinner one evening that fall that Richard first saw the white hart by the shimmering pool. There was a splash in the water, and suddenly, in the fading light, he caught a glimpse of a white haunch, a flash of leg, a dart of head before the startled stag leaped into thick brush. But there was still enough daylight left for Richard to feel sure of what he had seen. A *unicorn*. What else but a unicorn was that silken swift and dazzling white?

Recognition, almost like a pain, burned in his heart.

All the things that he had ever read about unicorns tumbled into his mind. That they had been confused with rhinoceroses. That sailors brought back narwhale tusks and said they came from unicorns. That the early Christians thought the unicorn a symbol of Christ. He especially remembered the line "And He was beloved like the son of the Unicornes" because once he had tried to put it into a song in his own off-key way.

Richard shook his head to clear it of the tag-ends of his readings. He disliked the sudden leaps that his mind sometimes took. They were so untidy. He was more comfortable when he could set things down straight, in ordered lists as his father had.

Something in the back of his brain was bothering him, though. Some piece of the puzzle did not fit.

He rehearsed the scene again. The flash of haunch, leg, head. The startling white in the fall setting. The spiraled horn.

No. That was it. He had seen no horn.

The shift back into an ordinary day was too much to bear. Richard tried to shake off the disappointment. He ordered his thoughts, trying to control them. Made a mental list and read it off carefully. And then he made another connection. A unicorn was probably related to a deer. And if that was so, then perhaps it lost its horn every year just like a deer and grew a velvety one anew. He didn't recall reading such a thing in any of his father's books. But what did that matter? The answer felt right, it had to be right. He would take the books out of the study again and reread them, all the books that mentioned unicorns.

For it *was* a unicorn—of that Richard was once again convinced.

He hurried back to the great house, eager to get to his father's book-lined library. The beat of his heart paced his steps, and when he ran into the house his aunt could only raise her pencil-arched eyebrows and breathe out a surprised "Well!"

Richard did not let his aunt's eyebrows or her frequent "Well's" bother him. It had been five years since she and her husband had become his guardians. And for four of those years Richard had been too ill to care about raised eyebrows. He had just floated in the sea of his bed, his books his raft.

"Well, hello," Richard said back now, in unconscious parody, as if bursting breathless into the house were a usual entrance for him.

"Well! You were out until dark," she said, eyebrows lifting again in a kind of greeting.

Richard said no more but went into his father's study. It was kept just as his father had left it. A gentle widowed scholar and teacher who had died as quietly as he had lived, Edward Plante had left only his book-lined study as a legacy for his boy. The house and everything else had gone as a sort of bribe to his younger brother and sister-in-law to take care of Richard. Whenever Richard felt tired or mean, he would think bitterly that the arrangement had worked very well. Hugh Plante and his wife had moved in just in time to give Richard into the hands of a doctor and to nurse him through his long days of sickness.

But most often Richard didn't feel mean, and lately

less and less tired. Still, he had never quite gotten over a certain distrust of his aunt and uncle. He felt, in the deepest part of him, that they were there because of the house and he was just another part of it, another part to be kept clean and polished and presentable.

In the study that was his but which he still called his father's, Richard went over to the middle shelf. It was the shelf he had practically learned by heart. Here were his favorite books. Folklore. Bestiaries. Collections of the Brothers Grimm and Asbjörnsen and William Butler Yeats. Fables and the fabulous. It was all there, all waiting for him to unriddle.

He put his hand out and reached for his father's well-thumbed copy of Robert Graves' *The White Goddess.* Richard had not yet understood more than the smallest part of it. But it was great poetry, he knew, and as he learned more he would understand more. He looked up *unicorn* in the index.

"Richard!" It was his aunt again. "Don't you ignore me, young man. Into a hot bath with you. Then bed. You might get sick all over again. Then where would you be?"

"Where would *you* be?" Richard thought. He knew where he would be—in bed. But what his Aunt Marcie really couldn't stand was the thought of all that waiting on him again. He had overheard her saying it to Uncle Hugh one day. And that's where she'd be, his aunt, who always seemed to intrude on him when he wanted to be private. She meant well, he tried to tell himself. It was just that she and his uncle seemed to consider silence a personal affront, an antisocial attitude on his part that they felt duty-bound

to change. So they tried to surround him with spoken words. He much preferred the quiet of the printed page.

Reluctantly but obediently, Richard went upstairs. The hallway was dark and Richard remembered how he used to dread the trip upstairs when he was little, even when they carried him up trailing his quilt. He had to admit that he still felt a bit queasy about walking through the dark. And though he no longer woke at night shrieking, oppressed by the dark weight on his chest, he still felt safer in the light. Of course he would never admit that to anyone, especially his aunt and uncle. He hardly liked to admit it to himself. So he squinted his eyes and barreled ahead, full tilt up the steps and into the bathroom. The contrasting glow of the lights was instantly comforting. He ran the bath as hot as he dared and sank down until only his nose showed. His body was underwater but his thoughts were still in the forest, where, with a flash of haunch and head, the unicorn danced on and on.

Richard knew what he must do. Morning, tomorrow being a Sunday, would give him plenty of time.

three

Heather Fielding was an enjoyer. She enjoyed other people, she enjoyed her family, she enjoyed new places, she enjoyed old legends, and she enjoyed slipping off quietly by herself on an adventure.

Since she had been little Heather had enjoyed going off alone. But she had an annoying habit of going too far and getting lost. About the third time the local police had been called out to find four-year-old Heather, the Fieldings began to keep a very careful eye on their only daughter. And even though she was now almost thirteen, she still had literally to sign out for an afternoon when she wanted to disappear. It meant leaving a detailed note on the bulletin board for her mother or three brothers. It was one of those many rules she had first resented and then found

ways to make enjoyable. And so this day the bulletin board read:

Don't have time to really stop.
Into Five Mile Wood on Hop.

Hop was Heather's horse, an appaloosa gelding, gentle and undemanding, with a gray-dappled hide that looked as if it had been spotted by raindrops. His slow, loose-limbed pace fitted Heather's style. It gave her plenty of time to enjoy, to drink in the world as they ambled by.

The fall day Heather saw the white deer, the sky was overcast and threatening. This only heightened her enjoyment, for the woods always changed colors under a leaden sky. Little creatures began to creep out that might otherwise have hidden, terrified of the bright, revealing sun.

Heather reined in Hop and slid off his broad back. She allowed the horse to wander and graze, knowing he would not let her out of his sight.

Then she sat down by the shimmering pool. Strangely, it was new to her. In all her wanderings she had never made the precise series of turns that led through the old apple orchard to here. It was a find. Heather breathed in the air. It was heavy, as heavy as the day. But it didn't make her feel unhappy. Nothing by this new discovery, this crystalline pool, blue and still, could make her feel sad.

She picked up a palm-size rock and flipped it over and over in her hand. It was cool and smooth; a faint gray-white line wormed its way across the rock's surface.

Heather flung the rock into the pool in order to watch the ripples. At the splash, another sound, a high whistling, started up from below the wild apple tree to her right.

There was an explosion of white head and flank. The dark hooves and horns were invisible against the brush, so gleaming white was the hide.

Heather leaped up at the same time, as startled as the deer.

"An albino," she breathed, and then was still. The beauty of the animal burned itself into her eyes. She blinked. The deer was gone. She closed her eyes. The image of the white hart seemed imprinted on the inside of her eyelids.

The animal's sudden, crashing flight broke across the stillness of the pond. As though a spell had been broken, the pond itself was ruffled by a breeze and a hound bayed from far off. The mood changed. Heather felt it was impossible to

13

stay any longer. But she repeated "An albino" to herself as she swung a leg over Hop's broad back.

She kept rehearsing the scene to herself and paid no attention to the road. The horse, without being guided, brought them both safely home.

Heather dismounted and settled Hop in the barn as if in a dream, for her thoughts were still back at the pool. Only the fact that her arms and legs knew the routine of feeding and bedding so well saved Hop from a long, cold, hungry night.

Entering the bright yellow kitchen, Heather was awakened by the smells. Saturday-night stew again. The famous Fielding leftover pot. As always on Saturday, they ate late, gathering in the scattered clan from the holiday tasks and events.

Heather debated telling of the pool. Usually her tongue ran ahead of her brain and she spoke without considering the consequences. Brian, her oldest brother, would often knot her long braids under her chin and say "You're tongue-tripping again." It might sound mean to someone outside the family, but Heather knew that Brian said it with affection.

Still, because the white hart had so captured her imagination, Heather hesitated about mentioning the pool to her family. The pool would lead them right to the white deer, and she could not tell them about that. Her brothers were all hunters. Nineteen, eighteen, and sixteen, they had had guns as long as she could remember. A shudder went through her as she pictured the white hart, crumpled and bleeding, on the forest floor.

No, this was one time she could not say anything to the family. Not even to her father, Julian, whom she adored.

And glancing guiltily around the table at the faces of those people she most dearly and truly loved, Heather resolved herself to silence. In fact, she was so quiet throughout the meal, it was noticed.

"Come on, Heath, where's your tongue?" It was Brian.

Dylan added, "She must be sick."

"Am not."

"Are, too." It was Ian. They always argued.

"Am not."

"Then why are you so sickly silent?"

"I'm just thinking."

"Come on, Heath. You *never* think."

"Mama." It was a plea.

"Children, children. Her silence is a blessing. Why not give me a wholesale blessing," said Mrs. Fielding, not having to add that Heather was the brightest one of the lot and well they all knew it, though her school work never reflected it.

"Amen," said Julian Fielding with such a hearty sigh that they all had to laugh. Even Heather. They left her alone after that as they talked about the hunting season to come.

In her silence, with the conversation so ordinary and familiar eddying about her, Heather planned what to do. Tomorrow, after church, there would be plenty of time.

· four ·

When the striped rock hit the water, the white hart leaped from his bed without thought.

As he ran down the path, his body gleaming in the twilight, he looked like a statue in motion. Under his gleaming coat the muscles rippled. The dark antlers, curving in a wide arch over his head, were a large, bony crown, all but invisible in the dusk. The brow tines were long and straight, and above them sprouted the bay tines, slightly curved. A third pair grew higher, with little fingers of horn on the spatulate tines.

The first fear gone, the white hart slowed down and began to feel hunger gnawing. Even though it was fall, there was still much rich food in the forest. Groves of young birch offered leafless shoots where he might browse, to grow fat against the coming winter. And there were acorns hidden in the mossy caves between the rocks or under the rotting leaves.

Far away, the hart could hear the baying of hounds. They were upwind, tracking some small animal across the meadow. It was a motley pack of farm dogs, led by a Scottish deerhound whose master never kept him tied. Abruptly the baying stopped. The quarry was caught.

The hart knew the pack was too far away to fear, and so he kept up his search for food. But as he looked for the shoots and nuts, the sounds of water called to him. There was a small stream nearby, tumbling over rocks, into riffles and pools of standing water filled with fish.

The hart went over to the stream, through a chest-high stand of dried sunflower disks that rattled crisply as he passed. He looked up the stream and down, then walked in. Pushing against the current, he came at last to one of the pools that was deep enough for him to stand in, and let the water swirl about his body.

He bathed then, going down first onto his knees and then rolling over, frightening the fingerlings and sending them fleeing in all directions.

Then he rose and walked out of the pool, upstream against the current, and onto the mossy bank. He shook himself all over and then rolled again, drying himself on the bank.

The hart stood up and raised his head, with its rack like a giant crown. He sniffed the air. There was no more danger. The intruders had left. Slowly he made his way back to the path, circled carefully for almost a mile, eating as he moved. But always he knew that he would return to the shimmering pool and his bed before morn.

· five ·

Richard woke up early enough to avoid his aunt and uncle. Sunday was their sleeping day. It was always a special day for Richard, too. He could have breakfast and the whole early morning to himself without their annoying questions.

For Aunt Marcie and Uncle Hugh always wanted to know *why*. Why don't you go out and play with other boys? Why can't you sit up straight at the table? Why do you read all the time? Why don't you ever want to talk about your father and mother? Why do you make those indecipherable lists? Why do you stare into space? Why? Why? Why?

All those questions were impossible to answer because the only reasons Richard could give them, they refused to accept: I am just me. It's just the way I am. Just because.

19

He wondered over and over how they could have known his father and not recognized that Richard had the same insatiable need to know, to understand, to study, to put bits of information in order. Richard wondered at their obtuseness. It was a good word, "obtuseness": dull and blunted. It seemed strange that his uncle should not be like his own brother, should not understand Richard at all. But then, they didn't really need to understand him, if they would just leave him alone. But they didn't leave him alone. They both kept asking Why? Why? Why? So Richard had stopped giving them his reasons, had virtually stopped talking to them beyond answering grunts at the breakfast and dinner table. And all they did was add a new question to their list. Why don't you talk to us? Why? Why? Why?

Richard went downstairs as quietly as he could, given the amount of clothes he had bundled on. If he was going to spend all day in the woods, he had to be sure to keep warm. Two pairs of socks, long johns, and two undershirts under his heaviest clothing. An extra sweater to carry along, just in case. Not to mention the jacket, mittens, scarf, and hat he was going to wear.

Breakfast was a quick snack of cheese and raisins. He packed a couple of peanut butter and apple jelly sandwiches in case, and stuck them in the jacket pocket. He did not know how long he would be gone. It might be all day. And if it *was* all day, he did not want his stomach talking to him in loud growls.

He did not even take a book, for he had sneaked down with a flashlight to his father's study after Uncle Hugh and Aunt Marcie had gone to bed. He had been up much of the night reading. He had read again all the references to unicorns in the folklore books. He had read from Ctesias, a Greek historian of the fourth century B.C. He had read a passage he had not understood at all in *The White Goddess* about a deer and a unicorn in the forest. He had checked *The Bestiary* by T. H. White and the encylopedias of mythology. And he had even borrowed one of Uncle Hugh's hunting magazines from the bathroom bookshelf and read it.

He felt that he now knew what he needed to know about unicorns. He had taken notes on all that he had read. Neatly written on 3 x 5 cards in his private code, they were now in his jacket pocket, nestled next to one of the sandwiches. Facts. Legends. Lists. He was as organized as he could be for seeing and understanding the beast. Beyond that . . . the pain in his chest came swiftly as it sometimes did when he was excited, a quick burning that went as fast as it came. Beyond that, he did not plan, for he did not dare. What could one do with a unicorn? Look at it and long for it, and love it. It was enough for now.

The door clicked behind him quietly. As he walked down the road toward Five Mile Wood, he finished dressing. He buttoned his jacket and wrapped the maroon scarf loosely around his neck. An old stocking cap of bright red yarn fitted over his mousy hair and stopped just short of covering his ears. They were always difficult to cover, his ears—they stuck out so. The gloves were from two different pairs, one of green wool and one of tan leather. The mismatch of color and material bothered him, and he kept his eyes off his hands, but he could not help feeling the difference. He hadn't had time to make a more thorough search. He was afraid that his aunt and uncle would be getting up soon.

As Richard walked along, his breath came out in short, wispy gusts, clouds of panting. The morning seemed to dare him. He took the dare and began to jog along. He could feel the sandwiches keeping time, hitting his sides in a soggy rhythm.

When he got to the turnoff into the woods, he stopped and looked around. The road was clear. No one was in sight, for it was still too early for the main church traffic. The Sunday silence, the early fall silence, lay over all. With a big smile, Richard plunged into the brush.

Within twenty minutes he had rediscovered the shimmering pool. He came upon it almost unexpectedly, after a last turn in the apple orchard. He had thought it was farther on, and to find it there, so close, was a shock.

There was no unicorn that he could see. But he hadn't expected to find it at once. That would have been too lucky, and Richard didn't believe in that kind of luck for himself. He was going to have to remain, in the words of the hunting book, "still and silent." It might be a long wait.

He found an inviting spot not far from the wild apple tree. He settled himself on the ground, sitting on the extra sweater to keep out the cold. Taking the sandwiches from his pocket, he found the cards, too. He spread them around where he could see and read them over and over but would not have to pick them up. He forbade himself any movement.

Today he would just *see* the unicorn. He would think about the rest later. But as he sat still, his thoughts began to drift to next week and beyond. Without a book to lead him on, for once he let himself be led by his own desires. And what he really wanted—he was beginning to understand it now—what he really wanted was to capture the unicorn. Not to hurt it, of course. Not to cage it. Just to tame it to his hand. His. His very own hand.

But from his reading Richard knew that the unicorn could be a dangerous beast. Its horn, its hooves, were lethal. So Richard had a problem to solve. In this time of still waiting, he would devise several plans.

One book—he found the card with his eye—told how to catch a unicorn by provoking the animal to charge. Then the hunter would dodge behind a tree and the beast's horn would become lodged in the tree. Once held fast that way, the unicorn was said to be easy to capture. Richard remembered the picture some ancient artist had made; it had been in the book, too. It was an interesting plan, to be sure. But he was not positive such a trick would work. For one thing, what if he couldn't outrun an angry unicorn? Or for another, what if it merely came 'round the tree? More important, a friendship shouldn't begin in anger. And he wanted the unicorn—rare and magical—to be his friend.

Another card caught his eye. He translated his code with practiced ease: "A pure Maid need only sit in the wood and the unicorn would come and place its head gently on her lap. Then she would secure it with a golden bridle and lead it like a pet out of the forest."

Richard was dubious. It might work. But there were two problems. The gold bridle was one. And the pure Maid. That was the other.

Richard puzzled over this and other problems for about two hours. Then the lack of sleep, the fresh air, and dreams overcame him. He fell asleep, still sitting backed up to the tree by the shimmering pool.

· six ·

Heather could barely sit through the church service. Usually she enjoyed the movement, the singing, the feeling of community, and especially the color. The light filtering through the stained-glass window where the lion and the lamb lay beneath Christ's feet always filled her with a special joy. But this Sunday was not like other Sundays. She didn't want to be enclosed in the church. Today it seemed airless, the dwelling place of men and not God's house.

The lion and the lamb kept reminding her of the woods outside. Her woods. She had always considered them so, ever since she was little. And especially Five Mile Wood, the meadows and the valley across from the state forest. Her brothers used it, bent the paths and trees and animals to their own needs. But she never *used* the woods. She let the woods become a part of her. And so she believed she and the woods were one, in some mysterious way. It was, she thought with sudden guilt at the blasphemy, a true eucharist. Body of my body, blood of my blood. My woods.

And outside in her woods, she knew, the white deer was waiting. Her deer.

"And he *is* mine," she thought fiercely. No one had ever mentioned the deer before, so no one else knew. It was that simple, that clear. And since keeping secrets was so difficult for Heather, for they always seemed to spill out of her, this secret had to be sworn in church.

She knelt down with the rest of the congregation but did not listen to their responses. She was repeating her own prayer over and over. "Please let me keep the secret. Please let me keep *this* secret."

She mumbled it loud enough for her brother Ian to knife her with his elbow. She shut her mouth and eyes and ears to the rest of the service and dreamed of the woods.

By the time the Fieldings returned to their home, it was lunch. Heather gulped her sandwich down so quickly she got the hiccups. Not wanting to ride while hiccuping, she had to waste precious minutes eating a teaspoon of sugar (her mother's idea), holding her breath (her father's idea), drinking a glass of water with a pencil clenched in her teeth (Dylan's contribution), and then nearly dying of fright when Ian jumped out at her from behind the staircase. Whether it was one or all of them together that worked, the hiccups were gone by the time she came out of the house.

The Transfigured Hart

"The message still stands," she had called back over her shoulder to Brian, who was going out of the barn. He would interpret her shout to the rest of the family: The note on the bulletin board was the same for today. So they all knew that Heather was going to be in Five Mile Wood, but they didn't know just where.

Heather got Hop from the barn and mounted him bareback, as usual. She resisted the temptation to kick him into a canter, for she knew that such a change from her usual slow, easy pace would bring a bevy of questions at the dinner table that evening. Then, deciding she must already have made them suspicious by her hasty exit from the table, she pressured Hop's broad ribs with her knees.

Once on the macadam road, she relaxed, and smiled at the thought of the albino. Her deer. Given enough time, quiet time, she could tame him. Of that there was no doubt. She knew she was good with animals. Her horse followed her everywhere. She had a dog, now too old to go far from home; three cats; a guinea pig; and two rabbits about to become more. She had, in turn, tamed a raccoon, a family of chipmunks, and surprisingly, even a black snake. And she had entertained her family in the evenings with tales of her progress. Taming the deer might take longer. Or shorter. You never knew with a wild animal. But the challenge called to her.

She turned Hop into a path lined with Sweet Everlasting, the white flower clusters still fragrant despite the cold fall. The path led through the old apple orchard and into the heart of Five Mile Wood.

27

When they got to the pool, sooner than she had expected, Heather slid off Hop's back. Holding his halter, she led him around the water. Today she wanted to tie him in one place, where he could graze quietly but would not frighten the deer when he came. For the white deer would come back. She knew this for sure. As the only non-hunter in a family of hunters, Heather knew that deer had special eating and drinking and sleeping habits. They rarely went more than a mile or two away from their own territory.

She led Hop silently, looking up at the sky to check the time and weather. That was why she did not notice the sleeping boy until she tripped over his outstretched foot.

Straightening herself quickly, she looked down at him. "Who are you?" she demanded, louder than she meant. "What are you doing at my pool?"

Richard woke with a start to see a skinny girl standing over him. Behind her was a spotted horse. Framed against the sky, they looked enormous.

"What? I mean, who are *you*?" he shouted in return, his voice breaking on the last word as he jumped up to face her. Once on his feet, he could see she was actually small, smaller than he by half a head.

"Who are you?" she flung back at him.

"You first."

"I asked first."

"What does that matter?" He suddenly stopped shouting and added, in a hissing whisper, "Shhh."

Heather quieted, too, suddenly remembering the deer. "It matters because . . . oh, damn you." Tears started in her eyes. The white deer secret, so beautiful and special and hers alone, was spoiled. She made a face to help control the tremble of her mouth, but the anger shaking her would not go away. Bending down, she picked up a forked stick and flung it savagely into the underbrush. It fell, with a soft thud, by the apple tree.

seven

The white hart could hide no more. He started up with a shrill whistle and leaped away.

All either child saw was his white tail and legs as he disappeared into the thicket.

Once away from the danger, the white hart began a browsing search for food through a piney wood. All that afternoon, he kept well below the shoulder of the hills. His instincts were good, for his outline would not show up against the sky.

Occasionally he stopped by a stream to drink deeply of the cold, clear water. Mostly he followed the barely discernible trails that he had worn away over five years. They were his paths, often running parallel with, but not touching, the trails that had been known and followed by generations of other deer.

The afternoon was closing down, making shadows dance in the feathery pines. Yet the shadows did not frighten the white deer as he moved purposefully through the woods.

He paused at the last line of trees, grown many branchless feet high, their tops full, and green. The needles were soft underfoot and silent, but occasionally he crunched a tiny pine cone as he made his way to the wood's edge.

Beyond the pine forest lay a meadow, quite brown and sere, for the fall had been exceptionally dry. At evening, the hart could make out the movements of a herd of does near the far side. There were seven, and with them five fawns and several yearlings. Close by and yet not too close were four bucks, in pairs. It was no longer the time of rut, and so the pairs of bucks remained together, apart from the herd.

Each pair consisted of an older male with a younger. They regarded the does with only a mild interest and then passed them by. They would seek their own food farther on.

From the forest edge the white hart watched the slow-paced ritual of does and bucks. That he was a deer made him part of them, yet he was separate. He did not seek any of them, they did not accept him.

The setting sun went down entirely behind the mountains and the meadow was suddenly dark. The white hart moved his head, sniffed the air, turned, and was gone.

Not one of the other deer remarked his leaving.

· eight ·

"Now you've done it," said Richard angrily.

"*I've* done it?" Heather's body was rigid. "You've done it. Shouting like that. You've scared my white deer away."

"You were the one who threw the stick. You were the one who came clomping in here while I was quietly waiting. I've been waiting since this morning. And what do you mean *yours*? And what do you mean *deer*?"

It was a long speech for Richard, and made to a stranger. The effort seemed to exhaust him. He sank back down again on his sweater, chin between his knees.

"Hold on," said Heather. She was used to dealing with boys who shouted and stood up to her. She was not sure what to do about one who started collapsing after the very first encounter. "Okay. I admit it. I was pretty noisy. And I admit I threw the stick, too. But what are you doing here, anyway? You weren't waiting. You were sleeping. And what do you mean 'what deer?' Why, the white deer, of course. The albino. The one that just jumped up and ran off. You saw him, too. Don't try and tell me you didn't." It seemed suddenly important that the boy not deny this, though moments before she had wanted the deer all to herself.

Richard looked up at her warily. She was an intruder. She was a loud, angry intruder in this place of peace. But still, she had seen it. And called it a deer. He had to tell her what it really was. She knew about it anyhow, that it existed. She had to know its true name.

"It's not a deer," he said. "It's something more beautiful. It's a unicorn."

"You're crazy," she said and started to walk away.

"No, wait." He jumped up again and came over to her. "Don't go away. Let me explain. I know it seems strange. But I've been studying about it, the unicorn."

"Unicorns don't exist," said Heather. "And maybe you don't exist either. Sleeping on sweaters with . . . with . . ." She noticed the cards fanned out around the apple tree. "With litter all over the place. You're crazy."

"Wait, please," he said. The last word came out as a special request, for Richard seldom said "please" to anyone. He either did something or he didn't. But he hardly ever asked, for asking always seemed to lead to more questions. "Did you see a rack? I mean antlers. If it was a deer, you would have seen them."

"I know what a rack is," said Heather. "And of course I did." Then she stopped and looked down. Her braids swung back and forth. Lying was something she just couldn't do. Her honesty was what made her an easy target for her brothers, though she didn't realize it and couldn't have changed if she did. Her hesitation made Richard bolder.

"You didn't, did you?"

"Well . . ."

"Well, did you?"

"I never saw him slowly. Or closely," Heather admitted. "I mean, he was mostly just a bunch of white. And the antlers would be dark, anyway. So maybe I wouldn't have seen them with all the white." It sounded lame, even to her.

"So you can't say for sure it was just a deer," Richard said.

"Of course it was a deer; what else could it be?"

"I *told* you," Richard answered. "It's a unicorn."

"You're crazy."

"But you didn't see any antlers."

"You're crazy."

"And deer aren't that white, that gleaming, that . . . that beautiful."

"Oh, they're beautiful, all right." Heather was definite. "There's nothing more beautiful than a deer in the wood."

Richard went on as if he had not heard. "And the pool where a unicorn drinks is clear and blue and quiet. It is free from all poisons, because the unicorn dips its horn there. And all little animals are safe there. But if the unicorn leaves, or is driven away, the pool turns bracken. Like a swamp."

"You *are* crazy."

Richard turned then and looked straight at her. "This pool and that animal we both saw were different from any we have ever seen." He ached to explain it in just the right way. "Just to look at the pool and the beast, you knew how different."

"Well . . ."

"And it made *me* feel different, too. Important. No, *special.* Because I was allowed to see it when no one else did."

"I saw it."

Richard ignored her. "And inside me, it was like something that had been holding me had burst, like a chain had snapped. And something else, too. I felt . . . I felt I had always been a puzzle with pieces missing and now the pieces were all there, had been given to me, and all I had to do was put them in the right places. Only just when I was going to put them together, *you* came." He looked up at her again, but not with bitterness. It was just an assessment he was making, painstakingly judging each word before dealing it out. It was as if nothing was true until he spoke it aloud, and then it *became* true.

Heather responded immediately, for his hesitation seemed to beg for a response, and she was moved by the plea. "Yes," she said. "I know."

It was all the encouragement he needed. Almost wildly he said, "You know!"

"But it couldn't be. They aren't real. It couldn't be."

"It was," said Richard. "It is."

"A unicorn," Heather whispered, and then was still.

• nine •

"Tell me more about unicorns," said Heather, finally, flopping down beside Richard. She landed half on, half off his spread-out sweater. One of her sneakers scuffed at a card and left a dirty mark on it.

Richard hesitated a moment. He felt a great thudding in his chest and hoped he wouldn't be sick.

"Unicorns are *ughm.*" He cleared his throat of his voice, which had suddenly begun to squeak. "Unicorns were *ughm.*" The throat kept doing funny things. It was better when the girl had been an enemy. He took a deep breath and said, "I'm Richard Plante." As he spoke he moved away a bit.

"I know. The boy with the broken heart. You've just come to school. I've heard about you and seen you between classes. I'm Heather Fielding. We're almost neighbors."

"It's not broken. Just . . . just bruised a little." It was a feeble joke, but Heather suddenly burst into great gales of laughter as if she thoroughly enjoyed it. It was contagious and Richard joined in. They both laughed until they were exhausted, and then Heather suddenly rolled over on her stomach, full on the sweater, her braids coiling on the ground. Richard, in an awkward scramble, was pushed onto the cold ground.

Heather looked over at the boy. He seemed suddenly so uncomfortable—prickly or shy, like a wild animal unused to the touch of a human hand. She folded her hands together and was very quiet, as if to show him she wouldn't try to hurt him. Then she said again in a very tiny voice, "Tell me more about unicorns."

Richard checked her out from the corner of his eye. She had said the last with such obvious sincerity. He sighed. He would try his voice again. "The books all say the unicorn is a mythical beast." He looked down at her.

Heather continued to stare quietly at her hands. At last she said, "Is there only one of it?"

"I don't know," said Richard, at once bewildered at her leap and comforted by her interest. "I could look it up."

"Okay. But not now." She smiled, but the smile went into the ground, not toward Richard. "Now finish telling me about unicorns."

"I haven't begun yet."

Heather didn't say anything, and her silence encouraged him.

"The books say the unicorn is as old as Greek or Roman myths at least."

"At least," agreed Heather.

Richard looked over at her to see if she was mocking him. But she was just nodding and waiting for him to go on, plucking at some dry grass.

"It's supposed to look like a horse. Or a goat. Or maybe a deer. And it has this one golden horn in the middle of its head. A horn with a spiral twist."

"I like that," Heather said. "The twist, I mean."

"The name 'unicorn' means 'one-horn.' " Richard said it suddenly, almost triumphantly.

"I know that!"

"You do?"

"I'm taking Latin," said Heather.

This so surprised Richard that he didn't know what to say. Yet he didn't know why he should be surprised. So he ignored it and went on. "Some unicorns seemed to have goat's beards or lion's tails." He reached out to finger the card with the smudge on it.

"So there are—I mean is, or do I mean are?—more than one in the world."

Richard was puzzled again at this leap. Then, just as suddenly, he understood the way her mind had gone. He said thoughtfully, "I think it's just the difference between one storyteller and another. One added a tail. Another a beard."

"Okay," said Heather, plucking at the dry grass again, "but it might be important." She noticed the sandwiches wrapped up and lying on the ground. She sat up then and picked them up, offering one to Richard and taking the other herself. She began to munch, and then, with a mouth full of peanut butter and apple jelly, said, "You see, we have to know everything we can about it if we're going to tame it. If there's a herd, or if it's male or female, or what it likes to eat or . . ."

"But how did you know?"

Heather looked at him. "Know what?"

"That I want to tame it."

"*I* want to tame it."

"But it's my . . ."

"*Our* unicorn," said Heather. "So we will have to do it together. What do the books say about taming unicorns?"

"Well," admitted Richard, "they mostly say the unicorn can only be captured with a golden bridle by a pure Maid."

"We've got one of those at home," said Heather excitedly.

"A golden bridle?" asked Richard.

"No," said Heather. "The maid. Well, maybe not a maid, but a cleaning lady."

"Oh my God!" said Richard.

"What's wrong?"

"A Maid, a pure Maid is . . ." He suddenly stopped talking.

"Did I say something wrong?" asked Heather.

"A Maid is a maiden."

"Oh," said Heather, without thinking. "You mean a virgin."

They were both so embarrassed then, they flopped simultaneously on the grass, and their shoulders almost touched.

"Well," said Heather at last, "we do have one of those." She looked down steadily at the ground as if summoning up the courage to say what had to be said next. And then suddenly she sat up on her knees and looked at Richard, her eyes and mouth smiling. She drew in a deep breath. "Then *I* could capture it. It would still be mine. You couldn't, could you? I mean, I am. I am a Maid. And I can get the unicorn."

"It might be scary."

"I'm not afraid. Animals don't scare me. I've tamed a raccoon and a whole family of chipmunks and a snake."

"You have to sit in the forest and let it put its head in your lap."

"I'm still not afraid."

"Horn and all?"

Heather bit her lip. She had forgotten about that. Then she looked at Richard, who was watching her carefully. She nodded. "Horn and all."

"All right," he said.

They got up as if by mutual consent. Richard picked up the cards and the sandwich wrappings and stuffed them into his pockets. He tied his sweater carefully around his waist.

While he got ready, in silence Heather mounted Hop, leaping onto him with a light quick movement that surprised Richard.

Richard walked over to the horse and girl. Cautiously he put his hand to the horse's flank. It was warmer than he expected. The muscles under the skin flinched at his touch, but otherwise the horse did not move.

42

Heather squeezed Hop with her knees and he started his long, slow, rolling walk. Richard kept his hand on the horse and they walked that way until they got to the road. Then Richard went toward his house and Heather turned Hop around and went home.

· *ten* ·

The hart came home, too, to his bed of fern by the pool, but he did not come home until morning.

It was a strange pool, crystalline and blue, like a piece of polished sapphire. And it was strangely quiet, too, for birds did not call out idly there, nor did little animals scratch and scrabble wildly in the undergrowth.

The white hart settled himself down, nose to the ground. In the summer, his ears kept up a constant twitching as he tried to rid himself of the tormenting flies. But this late in the fall, the flies were mostly gone. So the white hart lay absolutely still.

He looked asleep, but he was alert. His eyes and ears and nose worked silently for him. The November night was cold. Soon there would be rims of ice on the lake and ponds, a snowfall of light powder to dust the trails. But until the deep snows of winter, when he would seek the sheltered creek bottom or the southern slope of Little Sugarloaf Mountain, this clear, strange pool was his special home.

The white hart sniffed the air again. The wind brought him the sweet pungence of pine and fern, and the late-blooming gentian; the sharper smell of several small animals upwind. But there was no danger his nose or ears warned him of.

He closed his eyes and slept.

· eleven ·

By mutual assent, though neither had said a word about it, Richard and Heather did not talk to each other at school. They did not show, by the flicker of an eye, that they even knew each other's names.

For Richard this meant no difference in his outward habits. He spoke to no one in his classes beyond answering direct questions or giving page references. As for Heather, her lighthearted talkiness just remained directed toward the crowd of girls that milled about her.

Once, as he passed by her that week in school, Richard was startled to hear her say "But I saw the deer . . ." and he stopped, unable to move farther down the hall, an emotion that was part anger, part fear, and part pure horror seething inside him.

An older boy bumped into him at that moment, and

Richard was thrown off balance. As he recovered, he heard the rest of the sentence: ". . . down in the far meadow by the piney woods. I hope my brothers don't find out. If they knew there are a lot of them, they'd be all over Five Mile Wood."

Richard felt the steel band around his chest snap, just like Faithful John in the fairy tale. Only he hadn't been faithful, he thought. He had thought Heather guilty of betraying their secret. Just because the word "deer" is both singular and plural. He couldn't wait until school was over and he could meet Heather at the shimmering pool. He wouldn't, couldn't, tell her what happened, but would be extra nice to her to make up for his suspicions.

They had been meeting at the pool every afternoon. Some afternoons, because she had lessons of one sort or another, Heather did not get there until late. But get there she did.

The first day, Monday, Richard had gone back on his own, fighting his fears and anticipations in equal measure. He had rehearsed the scene so often, it was as if it had already happened. Yet when it came, it was different from all he had imagined.

He had barely settled down when he heard some branches snap and the breathing of a large animal. It was too heavy and earthbound for the unicorn, of that he was sure. It had to be Heather's horse.

He jumped up in greeting. Heather waved gaily in return and slid from the horse's broad back. She tied the reins to a tree branch and came over. She would have taken Richard's hand, but he drew away and gestured awkwardly to the old army blanket he had spread on the ground. Heather shrugged and sat down, sitting cross-legged.

Richard sat down carefully on the far edge. "I hoped you would come," he began. It was how he had begun every scene in his mind.

"Couldn't keep us away."

"Us?" Richard was disconcerted, for in his rehearsals she had never said anything like that.

"Hop and me." She nodded at her horse.

"Do you go everywhere on that horse?"

"On Hop? Of course. Oh, he won't scare the deer, I mean unicorn, away if that's what's worrying you."

Richard looked down. "You don't really believe in it, do you," he said. It was a statement, not a question.

"No, I do. I really do. It's just . . . it's just it takes some getting used to. I mean, I've seen loads of deer, but I've never seen a unicorn before. And yesterday, when it was here—the unicorn—it seemed right. That it was a unicorn. I believed the whole thing. But today—today it seems harder, somehow, to believe."

"It takes practice."

It was Heather's turn to look bewildered. "What?"

"Believing. It takes practice."

"That's a weird thing to say."

"Well, actually, I didn't invent it. The White Queen said it."

"But that's Wonderland. And this is here." Heather said it softly. It didn't sound angry or unbelieving or anything negative. It sounded just as if she wanted to be convinced.

"Wait till you see the unicorn again," Richard said. "You'll believe it. I know you will."

"I know I will, too," said Heather.

"If your horse doesn't scare it away." Richard didn't know why he added that.

"Look," said Heather. She was clearly annoyed. "I told you he wouldn't scare it away."

"You said 'deer.' "

"Well, I meant 'unicorn.' And what do you have against my horse, anyway?"

Richard shrugged and looked over at the horse that was quietly cropping the brown grass. Occasionally the horse took a cautious step toward Heather and was stopped by the halter reins looped and knotted around the tree. "I don't . . . it's . . . his spots, I guess. Like measles. Or chicken pox. You know, diseases. Not white like the unicorn, but diseased. That's it. He looks diseased."

"Oh no," said Heather.

"You asked," Richard said defensively.

"But he's not spotted like a disease," she said. "You've got it all wrong. He's dappled like trout and finch's wings and freckles." She closed her eyes and recited: "Glory be to God for dappled things."

"But that's a poem," said Richard. "That's Gerard Manley Hopkins."

At his name, Hop lifted his ears and twitched them back and forth, whickering softly.

"Of course," said Heather. "Do you think you're the only one in the whole world who reads?"

Before Richard could begin to frame an answer, Heather reached into the pocket of her blue jeans and pulled out a crumpled piece of paper. "I was hoping I would see you today. No, I *believed* I would see you today." Her attempt at sarcasm fell flat and made them both uneasy, so they pointedly ignored it and Heather went on. "I copied this down. We have a book at home on the unicorn tapestries. I'll bring it tomorrow if you like."

Richard was eager to please her. "Yes, I'd like that," he said rather more formally than he intended.

Heather smoothed out the paper with fingers that still bore signs of her afternoon painting class. "It says that 'wealthy kings and bishops owned unicorn horns, long and whorled and white.' What's 'whorled'?"

"Twisted." He made an upward spiral motion with his hand.

" 'Five feet or more in length. These horns were beyond price, for they changed color when brought into contact with poisoned food or drink.' " Heather cocked her head to one side and thought a minute. "There must have been an awful lot of unicorns around."

"I don't know," said Richard. "Maybe then. But I like to think that there's just one in the whole world now."

"Yes," said Heather. "Ours."

Suddenly Richard had a horrifying thought. "How do you suppose the kings and bishops got all those horns?"

"I don't want to think about that."

"Could be the unicorns shed their horns every year like deer, and the kings and bishops just found the horns lying around under trees."

Heather grinned. "Medieval litter," she said.

"I used to call it," Richard said, trying out a joke of his own, "I used to call it the Middle Evils."

Heather clapped her hands delightedly.

Richard relaxed and allowed a grin to pull itself across his face. "What else does *your* book say?"

"Just the other stuff you said yesterday. About the Maid . . . maiden. Except . . ." Heather hesitated.

"Except what?"

"Except if she had any stain in her—the maiden—the unicorn would rip her open with its horn. I think that means if she isn't pure any more. But I'm not really sure how far . . . what a stain is. I kissed Henry Castlemain at his birthday party. It was just a game. Is that a stain?"

"Oh, I don't think so," Richard said quickly, furious at the thought.

"But then, you aren't a unicorn."

"Are you afraid?" Richard asked.

Heather considered the question a long time. She was remembering Henry Castlemain and trying not to think about the horn. It was some time before she spoke.

"If you were there with me, I wouldn't be afraid."

Richard smiled. "Of course I'll be there," he said.

· twelve ·

$\mathcal{E}$ ach subsequent meeting at the pool was a discovery. They discovered they both liked poetry, though Richard liked to read it silently and Heather to recite it aloud. They discovered they both liked fall better than spring— Richard for all the things that were being covered and hidden, Heather for the colors and the raucous calls of the birds flying south. They discovered they both liked secrets, though Richard had always known it and Heather had just learned it. And they discovered each other.

It happened on Friday, that final discovery, when Richard was walking Heather to her horse. "I never talk to anyone, and now I'm talking to you."

"Oh, I talk *to* a lot of people. And a lot of people talk *at* me," Heather answered. "But you're the only one I talk *with!*"

They were both silent a moment. Then, as Heather climbed onto Hop, they both started again in a rush.

"Why do you suppose we haven't seen . . ." Richard began.

"Do you think you might come to dinner tonight?" Heather asked.

The invitation was overriding. Not only was Heather's voice louder, but in the confusion and excitement, they both forgot Richard's question, which was the more important. For they hadn't seen the white hart since the previous Sunday when they had started him from his soft ferny bed.

Richard was alarmed at the idea of going to Heather's house for dinner, to face the barrage of questions she had promised him would come from her boisterous family; yet he blurted out "yes" without hesitation. His tongue was simply not listening to his cowardly heart.

Heather shouted, "Great! See you at six. Only white house on Hunt's Lane," and kicked Hop into a lazy canter before Richard could change his mind. Indeed, she could hear him shouting after her, "Wait, Heather! Maybe I shouldn't." She refused to hear any more.

Richard was so afraid of telephoning the Fieldings to say he couldn't come that he went. In fact, his Uncle Hugh drove him over and didn't stop talking the entire way, so there was never any time for Richard to voice his fears.

"Never really met the Fieldings," Uncle Hugh was saying. "But know them by sight. Good family. Stick together. Great hunters, too, you know. Been here generations, not newcomers like us. Own a lot of the town, or used

54

to. Understand she paints. Pretty woman. You meet the girl in school?" It went on like that for some time. So when they finally arrived at the only white house on Hunt's Lane, Uncle Hugh carried his monologue right into the house and finished it up on Mrs. Fielding.

She didn't seem to recognize it as one-sided. Presumably she had participated in many similar ones before. She invited him in for a drink.

Heather and Richard stared at each other for a long, horrible moment, suddenly strangers, and Heather ran back into the kitchen, where she attacked the salad with a paring knife. Richard wanted to follow her in and he wanted to run out to the car and he wanted to sink into the carpet. Instead he stood where he was, feeling sure that every time Heather's brothers, unseen in the family room, laughed at the television show they were really laughing at him.

At last his uncle's drinks and his uncle's jokes were finished. Uncle Hugh clapped him on the back and said, "I'll be back at ten for you," and disappeared out into the fresh night air.

At that point, dinner was served.

If dinner was good or bad Richard did not know. He barely ate it. Heather watched him turn alternately white and pink as the conversation eddied and flowed around him. She pitied him and was angry at him for not being as funny and dear and sweet and serious as she knew he was. Her brothers seemed especially loud in their jokes. Yet they also seemed lively, while Richard seemed dead or turned to stone.

"Richard and I," Heather said, "have known each other for ages. In school. But we never spoke until last week. Did we, Richard?"

"*Ughm,*" Richard said, the horrible noise rising again in his throat. The questions had started, and Heather herself had started them. He felt like an animal at bay.

"Richard, dear, you've scarcely touched your plate. Is anything wrong with the food?" That was Mrs. Fielding.

They were going to be on him now for sure, Richard thought. Why? Why? Why? There was no hope of avoiding the questions.

"Are you in Heather's class?" asked Mr. Fielding.

"A grade ahead, actually," said Heather, slipping in with answers to rescue him. He threw her a thankful look. "He was tutored and is ever so much smarter than the rest of us, aren't you, Richard?"

It was the kind of question that needed no answer, and they both knew it.

Ian looked up from his plate, where, until now, most of his attention had rested. He tossed his dark hair out of his eyes. "Richard? Or Dick? Or Rich? Do they really call you the whole thing—Richard?"

Brian, across the table, laughed. "Richard the First, Richard the Second, or Richard the Third?"

"Oh, don't be beastly," said Heather, grimacing across at him.

"Well, which is it?" asked Dylan. A natural athlete, he fancied himself a scholar as well, and was actually close to brilliant at history. "Richard the Third was a humpback, so that can't be it. You're tall but straight. And Richard the

First was lionhearted, brave, and outspoken. Or so they say. Whoever *they* is. They always say *they* when they don't have any real facts. But you don't seem very outspoken. How about lionhearted and brave? And Richard the Second was . . . well, he was a bit of a problem, he was. He had an overbearing uncle and a rebellion and a flag with a white deer on it. Which . . ."

"A white deer? Oh, Richard, then that one's you. It's our . . ." Horrified, Heather stopped herself by clapping both her hands over her mouth. She stared at Richard, who suddenly couldn't take his eyes off the table. He turned absolutely white himself and started to choke on his food.

"Hit him on the back," cried Ian.

Mr. Fielding, sitting at the head of the table, reached over and began to pound Richard while the boy kept on sputtering.

"Not so hard, dear, he has a bad heart."

"Only bruised, Mother," said Heather, but it didn't sound like a joke at all.

Brian, though, was not to be diverted. "What's this about a deer, Heath? Have you spotted one for us?"

Ian took it up. "Where'd you find it, Heath?"

Heather, her hands back again on her mouth, shook her head, imperceptibly at first, then harder and harder. But the boys would not let up.

"Heath's a great little spotter, Rich," Dylan said. "She and Hop find all our deer for us on their travels. She never wants to tell us where they are, but she never can keep a secret. We always worm it out of her in time."

"She has this peculiar problem, you see," Ian added.

"She cannot tell a lie." He put his hand up as if pledging allegiance. "So it's all a matter of asking the right questions."

Brian came in then. "The Famous Fielding Finder, we call her, don't we?"

"Boys," warned Mr. Fielding, who realized that this time the teasing had gone too far.

But Ian did not pay attention. Like a dog on the scent, he was unable to stop. "Hey, I know where you went this week. Bet it's in Five Mile Wood. Come on, Heath, is he big? Is he a nine-pointer? Don't forget, tomorrow's Opening Day."

Heather ripped her hands from her mouth and cried out, starting like a small animal from a bush, "It's a secret! I can't tell you. I can't. I can't. *Richard.*"

Richard pushed his chair away from the table and stood up. His arm brushed Mr. Fielding's wineglass and the glass overturned on the table, staining the cloth. He hissed at Heather, "Traitor. Traitor. You've just told them. You've just told them everything." His voice barely rose above a whisper, yet it could be heard clearly by everyone at the table.

Heather couldn't answer him. She felt he was right and yet he was wrong. She couldn't think what to do, and so she tried to buy time by reaching over with her linen napkin to sop up the spilled wine.

But Richard didn't wait for an answer. He ran to the door. He looked one more time at Heather, his mouth twisted with anger but his eyes brimming with tears. Then he opened the door and ran out of the house into the dark.

Heather couldn't move except to turn the napkin over and over, running her finger across the wine-colored stain. Suddenly her mother was standing by her chair with Richard's coat in her hands. "Best run after him, dear," she said. "He's very upset about something." And she handed Heather the coat.

"Oh, Mother," Heather said, snuffling, and then the sobs came in earnest. She let the coat slip through her fingers to the floor. Then she got up, went over to the door, and closed it.

· thirteen ·

The white hart slipped along the path, ever windward, between his bed and the feeding grounds. The path he chose was an old Indian trail through an orchard long gone to seed. Apples, sweet even without man's cultivating hand, could be found there in season. In season, too, wild blueberries lined the tumbled stone walls.

The hart's toes were still quite sharp. Age had not yet rounded them. They left small, precise prints in the soft parts of the path that a hunter might have followed.

This night, in the full moon, a keener hunter than man was on the hart's trail. The blue-gray Scottish deerhound was out tracking. Not one to go by scent, the rough-coated hound had glimpsed a shadowy movement through the moonlit trees and was on the hart's trail at once.

The dog had no real need of food. He ran home each evening for a dish set out by the door. But hunting wild deer was what he had been bred for. And the old blood called to him.

Usually the deerhound led a pack of farm dogs. But this night the others had remained home, chained or sleeping, content, their bellies filled with canned food. So the hound tracked the hart alone. A foolish joy, but one the dog could not deny himself.

The hart stopped in a small turnabout and sniffed the air again. He heard a crackling of twigs behind him. Instead of bounding away in swift leaps, the hart turned and set himself for a fight. He lowered his head slightly and pawed the ground.

The hound was not ready for such a trick. He bounded into the tiny clearing that was full of the overwhelming musk of deer. He nearly galloped right onto the hart's horns. The paleness of the animal, gleaming white in the half-light of moonshine, confused the dog for a moment.

That moment was all the hart needed. He scooped his head down and lifted the silent dog up upon his horns. The weapons of bone struck home.

Like a ghostly pantomime, gray and white in the wood, the deadly dance concluded. Speared, the dog was lifted into the air on the hart's rack. Only then, when he was in the air, did the dog begin to scream. He continued screaming as he was flung over the albino's back. He stopped only when he hit the ground, blood staining his gray coat.

The white hart paused a moment to pound the dog's crumpled body with his hooves. Then he turned and leaped off to find the shimmering pool—the fight, the death of the dog, already forgotten.

· *fourteen* ·

Richard felt a pain in his chest, but he did not stop and he barely noticed the dark. He knew he could not possibly run all the way home, but to keep warm he jogged slowly, willing the pain to go away. The rhythm, the pace, finally eased the ache, and it went, a little at a time. He was left with a feeling of exhilaration that surprised him. He guessed it was a combination of the crisp night air, the full moon, and the thought of what was to come. What had to come. People lay behind him; only the unicorn lay ahead. He would have to take action, something he had never really done before. It was like a quest, an adventure, a heroic journey. He could count on no one else in this, certainly not on Heather, who had betrayed them at their first real trial. He could count only on himself.

It pleased him that this time, he, Richard Plante,

would be doing this. Not reading about someone else in a book, hiding his fears in silent retreat from the world and its questions. He had the answer and he was giving it loud and clear.

As he thought, planned, what he had to do in the dark night ahead, a car flashed past him, the light suddenly blinding. Then the car turned and cruised up beside him.

Of course it was Uncle Hugh, phoned by the Fieldings. Richard slipped gratefully into the car's warmth. This was no compromise. He could do nothing until near midnight, when everyone was asleep.

Uncle Hugh did not speak, not when Richard got into the car and not later, when Aunt Marcie enfolded him in a hug calculated to drive out his demons.

For once Aunt Marcie was silent, too, except for her eyebrows, which worked up and down overtime. But Richard did not start any conversation, though he knew they were waiting for him to do so. Wordlessly, he went upstairs to bed.

He heard Uncle Hugh say, as he went up the dark stairs alone and totally unafraid, "He didn't say a thing. You'd think he'd have some explanation. I guess we'll wait till tomorrow and then we'll try and get his side of it." Richard could only guess at Aunt Marcie's eyebrows as she snorted in return "Young love!" and dialed the phone.

But none of it touched Richard as he marched up the stairs slowly and deliberately. He paused at the top landing and saluted the ghosts of his mother and father, whom he knew must hover somewhere in the house. Then he went into his room, closed the door firmly, and went to bed.

But not to sleep. No, not to sleep. For many long minutes, Richard waited for his aunt and uncle to go to bed. They would turn in early tonight. Uncle Hugh had never missed an opening of deer season yet, or so was his boast. The creak of the stairs, the shuffling in and out of the bathroom, the slight sighings and whisperings, the click of the closing door, were the signals Richard waited for. And after the noises ceased, he waited some more—twenty times sixty heartbeats—before he got out of bed.

He got up cautiously in case anyone was still awake. But his every move was ritual. He dressed in his good blue trousers and his blue jacket with the crest on it that Uncle Hugh had brought back from England. He put on his heaviest socks and boots. And for warmth, since he had left his coat at the Fieldings' house, he tossed his navy blue blanket around his shoulders like a cape. It hung in graceful folds to his ankles. Then he tiptoed down the stairs and out into the night.

The night was cold and crisp but windless. Richard walked briskly toward the path where he would turn off into the orchard. No cars passed by him as he walked, nor could he hear any of the usual night noises. There was just darkness and silence, heavy, palpable, and real.

In the daytime, coming down the path, he had often stumbled. But he did not stumble now. He walked with authority. And even the brambles, dried and stiff, did not catch his makeshift cape. He did not make a single wrong twist or turn or misstep, and he came at last to the shimmering pool watched only by the moon which hung like a blind eye in the blue-black socket of sky.

· fifteen ·

Heather leaned her back against the oak door. She looked straight ahead but could see nothing through her tears. No one in the family spoke to her, or if they did, she couldn't hear them. Snuffling faintly, she went up to her room.

She lay down on the bed and stared at the bright yellow canopy. When she had been much younger, she had played at being a princess in her room. But now it was as if the sky had fallen and was waiting, old and yellow, to crush her utterly. She turned over on her stomach and put her hands under her head.

It was then that she discovered she was still clutching the wine-stained dinner napkin. She raised up on her elbows and looked at it thoughtfully. She was still thoughtful when she took off her clothes and climbed into her

69

nightgown. It was long and white, with a shirring of lace and a yellow ribbon woven about the neck and a yellow tie at the waist.

Slowly she unplaited her braids. Her hair, so long bound, fell over her shoulders in dark shining waves and reached down to the small of her back.

Heather sat down again on the bed and smoothed the damask napkin on her lap. The red stain in the soft light of her room looked black, but it still had the sickly sweet smell of wine.

Heather shook her head vigorously, as if to shake off her imagings, and turned off the light. Then she lay down on the bed, tucked the napkin in her bodice, and remained unmoving in the dark.

A knock sounded on her door. Her mother came in. "Heather, dear, do you want to talk? Is there anything I can do?"

Heather willed her voice to calmness, firmness. "No, Mother. I'm all right. Really I am. We'll talk tomorrow. Please."

Mrs. Fielding knew her daughter well enough to leave then. Heather could hear whisperings in the hall. Her father and then the boys cursed Richard for a coward and a fool and asked about her. She knew her mother would make them leave her alone. At least until morning. Even so, that would barely be enough time for what had to be done.

For Heather knew that she and she alone had to act. And she had to act that night if she was to save the unicorn from the hunters—from her brothers and her father and all the rest. She could not count on Richard; he *was* a coward

and a fool, just as her brothers had said. A coward not to back her up, a fool to think she had let the secret slip on purpose. That she had, indeed, let the secret out was a pain she would have to bear alone. As penance, she would have to save the unicorn alone, too. So she waited out the ticking of her bedroom clock and kept herself awake.

The clock was barely touching eleven when the silence in the house told her everyone else was asleep. The boys and her father, she knew, always went to bed early the night before Opening Day. They had to rise before dawn. And her mother would be rising with them to fix them breakfast. It was a tradition never broken.

Heather got up and slipped her feet into boots. She moved silently downstairs, grabbed her heavy school cape from the closet, and was gone before the dog had time for more than a sleepy, growling yawn.

She did not take Hop out of the barn. He would hate to be disturbed for a night ride. And the heavy clopping of his hooves might alert someone in the house. Though she had to be back before one of the early risers noticed she was gone, silence was no less important than speed.

She ran down the road, her dark cape floating behind her like bat's wings, the white gown luminous in the dark. She was lucky that no cars passed as she ran. And when, out of breath and trembling slightly from the cold, she came to the path through the apple orchard, the moon came out from behind a cloud. It was full and bright, and in the shadows it cast, the linen dinner napkin tucked in her bodice glistened both white and black.

Heather was careful not to make a misstep as she went down the path toward the pool. She stepped on nothing that might crackle or snap. And when she came at last to the clearing where the pool was set like a jewel in a ring, Richard was there before her.

"You!" they said together. But in the single word was both surprise and forgiveness.

Richard hesitated, then took the blanket off his shoulders and spread it on the ground under the wild apple tree. They both sat down, hands folded, silent and waiting.

· sixteen ·

And then it came.

White and gleaming, stepping through fragrant sweet violets, the unicorn came.

It was high at the shoulder, with a neck both strong and thick. Its face was that of a goat or a deer, like neither and yet like both, with a tassel of white hair for a beard and eyes the color of old gold. Its slim legs ended in cloven hooves that shone silver in the moonlight. Its tail was long and fringed at the tip with hair as soft and fine as silken thread. And where it stepped, flowers sprang up, daisies and lilies and the wild strawberry, and plants that neither Richard nor Heather had seen before but knew at once, the cuckoopoint and columbine and the wild forest rose.

But it was the horn that caught their gaze. The

spiraled, ivory horn that thrust from the unicorn's head, that looked both cruel and kind. It was the horn that convinced them both that this could be no dream.

And so it came, the unicorn, more silent than night yet sweeter than singing. It came 'round the shimmering pool and knelt in front of the children as they sat breathless on the blanket. It knelt before them, not in humility but in fealty, and placed its head gently, oh so gently, in Heather's lap.

At the unicorn's touch, Heather sighed. And at her sigh, the silent woods around suddenly seemed to burst with the song of birds—thrush, and sparrow, and the rising meadowlark. And from far off, the children heard the unfamiliar jug-jug-jug of a nightingale.

And it was spring and summer in one. Richard looked around and saw that within the enclosure of the green meadow, ringed about with a stone wall, encircled in stone arms, was a season he had never seen before. The glade was dappled with thousands of flowers. He could see, from where he sat, pomegranate and cherry trees, orange and apple, all in full bloom. The smell of them in the air was so strong that he was almost giddy.

But Heather seemed to notice none of this. She had taken the yellow ribbon from her waist and bound it about the unicorn's head like a golden halter, over the forehead and around the soft white muzzle. Her fingers moved slowly but surely as she concentrated on the white head that lay on her lap, the horn carefully tucked under her arm. She stroked the unicorn's gleaming neck with her free hand and

crooned over and over, "You beauty, you love, you beauty." And the beast closed its eyes and shuddered once and then lay very still. She could feel the veins in its silken neck under her hand, pulsing, surging, but the great white head did not move.

Richard looked over at the beast and the girl, and on his knees he moved across the blanket to them. Hesitantly, he reached his hand out toward the unicorn's neck. And Heather looked up then and took his hand in hers and placed it on the soft, smooth neck. Richard smiled shyly, then broadly, and Heather smiled back.

As they sat there, the three, without a word, a sudden harsh note halloed from afar.

"A horn," Richard said, drawing his hand away quickly. "Heather, I heard a hunting horn."

But she seemed not to hear.

The horn sounded again, nearer. There was no mistaking its insistent cry.

"Heather!"

"Oh, Richard, I hear it. What shall we do?"

The unicorn opened its eyes, eyes of antique gold. It looked steadily up at Heather, but still it did not move.

Heather tried to push the heavy head off her lap. "You have to go. You *have* to. It must be near day. The hunters will kill you. They won't care that you're beautiful. They'll just want your horn. Oh, please. *Please.*" The last was an anguished cry, but still the unicorn did not move. It was as though it lay under a spell that was too old, too powerful to break.

78

"Richard, it won't move. What can we do? It'll be killed. It'll be our fault. Oh, Richard, what have you read about this? Think. *Think*."

Richard thought. He went over lists and lists in his mind. But he did not recall it in any of his reading. And then he remembered the unicorn tapestries Heather had found in her mother's art books. She had brought the book for them both to see. The unicorn had indeed been killed, slaughtered by men with sharp spears and menacing faces. What could he and Heather do about such evil?

Heather was leaning over the unicorn's neck and crying. "Oh, my beauty. Oh, forgive me. I didn't mean you to be killed. Before I saw you, really saw you, I wanted to tame you. But now I . . . we want to save you."

Richard watched her stroke the neck, the head, her hand moving hypnotically over the gleaming white, tangling in the yellow ribbon.

Suddenly Richard knew. "Heather," he shouted, "the yellow ribbon! It's the golden bridle. Take it off. Take it off!"

Heather looked at the ribbon and in that moment understood. She ripped it from the unicorn's neck. "Go!" she said. "Be free." The ribbon caught on the spiraled horn.

The minute the ribbon was off its neck, the unicorn got up heavily from its knees. It flung its head abruptly backward and the golden band flew through the air.

The ribbon landed in the middle of the pool and was sucked downward into the water with a horrible sound. The birds rose up mourning from the trees as, in a clatter of hooves, the unicorn circled the pool once, leaped over the stone wall, and disappeared.

In an instant it was November again, brown, sere, and cold.

And the pool was no longer crystal and shimmering but a dank, brackish bog the color of rotted logs.

· seventeen ·

The horn sounded again, only this ime it was clearly a car horn. Loud, insistent, it split the air over and over as the sun rose, shaded in fog, over the far mountains.

"It's day," said Richard heavily. "Opening Day."

"But it's all right," said Heather, soothingly. "The unicorn is gone. It's gone forever."

"How do you know?"

"I know because I believe. Even without much practice, I believe." Heather put out her hand to Richard and he took it. Then they curled together for warmth and fell asleep in the dawn.

They were found two hours later, still sleeping, by Brian and Ian, who signaled with three shots fired in the air. They had to be shaken awake, for somehow the gunfire did not disturb them. Wrapping themselves in cape and blanket, Heather and Richard stumbled groggily to their feet and followed the boys out to the road. The boys were rough with them, as if to punish them for the scare they had inflicted on the family and for the fact that they had ruined Opening Day.

When they got to the road, there was a long row of cars waiting, for hunters and police had joined in the search.

"Mom was worried and checked on you about midnight," Brian explained. "And when you were gone, she called Mrs. Plante."

Ian interrupted. "And when your aunt found out *you* were gone," he said to Richard, "that's when we really got worried, and called the police."

Dylan added, "Well, you can imagine the scene."

Heather and Richard could, indeed, imagine the scene. But they didn't speak. They just looked at each other, smiles hidden behind serious faces.

Mrs. Fielding came over and enfolded them at once. "It was silly to run away," she said to them both. "What happened at the table was nothing."

She smelled of talcum and early-morning coffee, and she seemed both angry and relieved. Richard breathed deeply, and for the first time since they had been found, spoke. "It wasn't 'nothing,' Mrs. Fielding. It was actually the beginning of something."

Mrs. Fielding did not answer. Perhaps she hadn't heard. Or perhaps she was afraid to ask what he meant, since they had been found sleeping together in the woods, Heather in her nightgown. But she was silent and just gathered them both in again, as she gathered all the arguments at her house, without judgment.

Heather allowed herself to be gathered in for a moment. Her chin went down on her chest, and the napkin tucked in her bodice tickled. She pulled it out and stared at it for a moment. It was no longer stained. It was white and fresh and gleaming.

"Look, Richard, look!" she cried, holding it up to his face. As it came close to him, Richard could smell the sweet scent of crushed violets, and faintly imprinted on the linen napkin he saw a pattern of swirls as if something spiral had lain there.

He sucked in his breath, and Heather tucked the napkin back in her gown, and without a word more they all went home.

There were explanations, of course. For a swamp doesn't appear and children disappear without them. But none of the explanations mattered to Richard and Heather. And they, alone, offered none in the general clamor that followed their midnight transfiguration. For indeed how could they explain about the unicorn? It was, after all, a mythical beast. Or the shimmering pool that had become a bog? Or the wine-stained table napkin now gleaming and white as the unicorn itself? They could think of no explanations that anyone would believe and so they smiled and gave none.

But they kept the napkin safe first in one drawer and then another, to remind them both, as if they needed reminding, of that moment in time when autumn became summer and now became then and what was logical and what was magical became one.

· eighteen ·

It was just dawn. The sun rose, shrouded in fog, and fog covered the valley.

The white hart ran swiftly and purposefully out of the woods. In the distance he could hear guns and the occasional bleat of a car horn.

He came to a wide macadam road which smelled sharply of men and machines and was covered with a rolling mist. He hesitated a moment, then clattered onto the hard surface.

The deer traveled east, toward the sun that burned behind its mask of fog. He ran for several miles, passed only by a single slow-moving car, but in the white fog he was almost invisible.

Suddenly he plunged into the brush on the opposite side of the road, turned around for just a moment, and

sniffed the air. His ears twitched forward and back. Then he moved into the low briars and disappeared.

The woods on this side of the road covered thousands of acres and were part of a protected reserve.

The white hart was never seen again.

Jane Yolen is the author of a growing list of distinguished books for young readers, including *The Girl Who Cried Flowers,* which was runner-up for the National Book Award in 1975. She has received many other awards and honors for her writings. Mythology, legend, and folklore have always fascinated her, and she has done a great deal of scholarly research in this area of literature; this special interest is often reflected in the themes of her stories, some of which reviewers have called "modern classics." After her graduation from Smith College, Ms. Yolen worked for several years as a children's book editor, but retired from this to devote more time to writing. She also teaches courses in writing books for children and is the author of a popular book on the subject. With her husband and their three young children, Jane Yolen lives in a lovely old farmhouse in Massachusetts.

Donna Diamond's exquisite pen-and-ink drawings for this book perfectly exemplify her belief that fantasy is best expressed through carefully rendered detail. She quotes Jean Cocteau, who said that ". . . wonderland has little use for vagueness, and that mystery exists only in precise things." A graduate of Boston University's School of Fine and Applied Art, Ms. Diamond has also studied at the Tanglewood Summer Art Program, the High School of Music and Art, and the School of Visual Arts in New York. In addition to art, she has also studied dance and still enjoys watching her favorite companies perform. She is married to a musician, and lives in New York City. This is the first children's book Donna Diamond has illustrated, though her work has already appeared in other publications.